DEDICATION

To the real Aidan, the original Wonder Kid. Keep soaring.
Love, Mom

DISCLAIMER

This book addresses food allergies and intolerances, which relate to the medical wellbeing of children. The contents of this book do not constitute medical advice and you should consult with your child's pediatrician on all matters pertaining to his or her health.

Please note that there is an important distinction between a food allergy and a food intolerance, although some symptoms can overlap. A food allergy involves an immune response and can be life threatening. A food intolerance involves a reaction stemming from the digestive system. Please see your child's doctor or consult a naturopath to help you decide how to best address the unique challenges your child has. A certified health coach may also help you in implementing elimination diets, meal planning, and specific food avoidance and substitutions.

COPYRIGHT INFORMATION

Aidan the Wonder Kid Who Could Not Be Stopped
A Food Allergy and Intolerance Story

© Colleen Brunetti, 2017. All rights reserved.
For permission requests, email bannonriverbooks@gmail.com

Illustrations, cover design, layout, and e-book formatting by Dan Carsten

Ordering Information: Special discounts are available on quantity purchases by corporations, associations, schools, libraries and others.
For details, send inquires to publisher email address above.

Published by Bannon River Books 97 Beechwood Farm Road, Rutland, VT 05701

Library of Congress catalog card number: 2017918023

ISBN – hardcover: 978-0-9908842-2-4   ISBN- paperback: 0-9908842-3-1

Printed in the United State of America

First Edition

AIDAN THE WONDER KID

WHO COULD NOT BE STOPPED!
A food allergy & intolerance story

Written by Colleen Brunetti
Illustrated by Dan Carsten

Bannon River Books
Rutland, VT

Aidan was a boy who loved many things.
He loved his Mom, his Dad, his baby
sister and his dog, Rocco, of course!

But he loved to DO things too...Lots of things!
He loved to read...He loved to dance.

He loved to build.

He even loved school (and recess best of all)!

And more than anything else in the world, Aidan loved to move. In fact, he had secret energy powers. He was . . .

AIDAN THE WONDER KID
WHO COULD NOT BE STOPPED!

When he ran, his feet barely touched the ground. When his family visited the ocean, he seemed to soar over the beach, his toes barely in the sand.

He almost never walked anywhere. What fun was walking when you could practically somersault your way through life? Why stroll into the living room when a front flip across the couch could get you there so much faster?

Rocco was Aidan's trusty sidekick. A boy and his dog, you know, are a mighty team indeed.

Together they would take over the backyard and go on grand adventures. Leap the playscape in a single bound.

Score a soccer goal to the roar of an adoring crowd. Race a bike up and down the roads so fast, they were barely a blur.

Rocco would get quite worn out. But Aidan? He would keep on moving, and running, and flipping, and loving life. That was what WONDER KIDS WHO COULD NOT BE STOPPED did!

Yes, being a WONDER KID was very good indeed. However, Aidan had a little problem. It seemed he got sick an awful lot. Much too often, something would suck those superpowers right out of him. His nose bothered him. His tummy bothered him. And his fevers bothered him.

On those days, there was no running, jumping, flipping, or scoring soccer goals in front of adoring crowds.

When Aidan was sick, it was no fun at all.

Thankfully, Aidan's Mom was awfully smart (as Moms often are!) and after some detective work, and a trip to a doctor, she figured out the secret answer to his troubles. It seemed that there were two little things that could take away Aidan's energy powers in one mighty swoop.

Things so small, so tiny, so unexpected, that if it weren't for SUPER SMART DETECTIVE MOM, they might never have been found at all. Those things were dairy and wheat!

A glass of milk could send Aidan from THE WONDER KID WHO COULD NOT BE STOPPED to a sniffley, drippy, fevery, icky, droopy boy who could barely muster a smile. A bite of bagel could leave his knees aching and his mood swirling like a thundercloud. Both made his tummy ache.

"No more wheat or dairy for you!" Mom said.
"Awwww, man!"

Now this was a bummer! What about pizza? What about ice cream? And OH NO, what about birthday parties? Was all the fun over?

Luckily, SUPER SMART DETECTIVE MOM had secret powers of her own, and she was quite the mad scientist in the kitchen. Together Aidan and Mom worked to find new foods to try. Ones that left him with all his super-energy powers, and not feeling droopy and sniffly with no fun at all.

As it turned out, Mom wasn't the only one who was awfully smart. Aidan was really smart too, and he quickly learned that when he fed his body exactly what it needed, his superpowers were better than ever.

Now he could run and jump and flip every day, and he almost never got sick anymore! So it was really okay by him if he had a special kind of no-milk ice cream at a birthday party or brought his own cake. He even learned to love tacos without cheese.

Aidan was also a **SUPER-DUPER TACO EATER** by the way!

Then something even more amazing happened. Aidan started to meet other kids who had to eat just right for THEIR bodies! And do you know what? Every single one of them had a different food that took away their superpowers. And every single one of them had their best superpowers when they fed their bodies just right.

Liam couldn't have gluten! Lily couldn't have nuts (and she carried a special magic wand just in case she came across some)! Jackson wasn't allergic to anything, but he sure felt his best when he cut down on the candy and ate more fruits and veggies!

And were they sad about it? Nope! No way! Not one bit! It seemed that if they ate just what their bodies needed – no more, and no less – then they could band together as THE WONDER KIDS WHO COULD NOT BE STOPPED.

And the fun was just beginning.

Dear Wonder Kid,

Did you enjoy this book? I hope you did! The illustrator, Mr. Dan, and I had a ton of fun creating it for you!

I'll bet you read this book with a grownup because there is a food that makes you feel sick, or you have a friend who has to be careful about what they eat. Am I right? Even if you don't know anyone right now, you will someday. Everyone's body needs different things to feel like a super hero!

I'm so glad you read this book, because now I get to tell you something really cool. I want you to know that you are super powerful too – just like Aidan and his friends! You have the choice every single day to choose healthy foods that make you feel your best!

For some kids, this means not eating a certain food that makes them sick. And for all kids, it means eating lots of healthy foods like fruits and vegetables every single day. Don't forget to drink lots of water too!

It's okay to have a treat now and then. But remember that to be a WONDER KID WHO CANNOT BE STOPPED, you also need to make good choices. Your body uses your food just like superpower fuel. And you want as much good stuff as you can get!

Have lots of fun trying new things and loving life!

~Ms. Colleen

Dear Grownups,

As you may have guessed, this story is (loosely) based on something that really happened. My vivacious and full-of-life son, Aidan, struggled with undiagnosed food intolerances for a few years. We didn't know why he couldn't keep weight on and was sick all the time. Every two or three weeks it seemed, he would come down with the sniffles that would lead to ear infections and fevers. We were stumped.

Luckily, just as we were coming to our wits' end, I was in the midst of my training as an Integrative Nutrition Health Coach. Throughout the course of my studies, I learned a lot about how food sensitivities can hide as seemingly unrelated health challenges.

After a visit to a naturopathic doctor who confirmed my suspicions, we took Aidan off dairy for six weeks. When we re-introduced it he got violently ill, and we knew we had our answer. Once he was off dairy, he went eleven months without so much as a cold. He also grew like a weed. Now that is a success story! We eventually removed wheat as well and saw behaviors and tummy issues dissipate.

This book is meant to help kids take ownership of feeding their bodies well, whatever that looks like, but there is an underlying message for you too.

You don't have to look far to see that our kids are really struggling with food-related issues. There are food intolerances like my son's. There are the more frightening food allergies that cause hives, anaphylaxis and emergency. Then there is the ever-rising tide of childhood obesity and illnesses such as asthma, allergies, and ADHD that can all be linked in some way to food.

The good news is that with diet tweaks and a little change in how we view foods, change and healing is possible. I would love to see your family have the same kinds of success we eventually found.

As a health coach, it is my passion to help support happy and healthy families and teachers. If you think your child could benefit from a change in eating, or if you just need some help learning to feed your family well so they can be the best they can be, I would love it if you got in touch!

Please visit my website at:
www.ColleenBrunetti.com to learn more!

I look forward to hearing from you!

Warmly,

Colleen Brunetti, M.Ed., C.H.C.

CPSIA information can be obtained
at www.ICGtesting.com
Printed in the USA
BVOW07*1500300118
506045BV00001B/1/P